Gary Gets a Gift

The Sound of Hard G

by Joanne Meier and Cecilia Minden · illustrated by Bob Ostrom

The Child's World

Published by The Child's World®
1980 Lookout Drive
Mankato, MN 56003-1705
800-599-READ
www.childsworld.com

The Child's World®: Mary Berendes, Publishing Director
The Design Lab: Design and page production

Library of Congress Cataloging-in-Publication Data
Meier, Joanne D.
  Gary gets a gift: the sound of hard g / by Joanne
Meier and Cecilia Minden ; illustrated by Bob Ostrom.
    p. cm.
  ISBN 978-1-60253-401-8 (library bound : alk. paper)
  1. English language—Consonants—Juvenile literature.
2. English language—Phonetics—Juvenile literature 3.
Reading—Phonetic method—Juvenile literature. I. Minden,
Cecilia. II. Ostrom, Bob. III. Title.
  PE1159.M456 2010
  [E]—dc22   2010002915

Printed in the United States of America in Mankato, MN.
July 2010
F11538

NOTE TO PARENTS AND EDUCATORS:

The Child's World® has created this series with the goal of exposing children to engaging stories and illustrations that assist in phonics development. The books in the series will help children learn the relationships between the letters of written language and the individual sounds of spoken language. This contact helps children learn to use these relationships to read and write words.

The books in this series follow a similar format. An introductory page, to be read by an adult, introduces the child to the phonics feature, or sound, that will be highlighted in the book. Read this page to the child, stressing the phonic feature. Help the student learn how to form the sound with her mouth. The story and engaging illustrations follow the introduction. At the end of the story, word lists categorize the feature words into their phonic elements.

Each book in this series has been carefully written to meet specific readability requirements. Close attention has been paid to elements such as word count, sentence length, and vocabulary. Readability formulas measure the ease with which the text can be read and understood. Each book in this series has been analyzed using the Spache readability formula.

Reading research suggests that systematic phonics instruction can greatly improve students' word recognition, spelling, and comprehension skills. This series assists in the teaching of phonics by providing students with important opportunities to apply their knowledge of phonics as they read words, sentences, and text.

The letter g makes two sounds.

The soft sound of **g** sounds like **g** as in: *giraffe* and *huge.*

The hard sound of **g** sounds like **g** as in: *go* and *gas.*

In this book, you will read words that have the hard **g** sound as in: *gift, game, good,* and *give.*

Gavin is on his way
to Gary's house.
He has a gift in his hands.

The gift is Gavin's favorite game. He thinks it will make a good gift.

Today is Gary's birthday.
Gavin is going to give
the game to Gary.

Gavin gets to Gary's house. He opens the gate to get to the door.

"Hi Gavin," says Gary.
"I'm so glad you could come over."

"What have you got in your hands?" says Gary.

"It's a gift for you," says Gavin.

"Happy birthday!"

"Wow!" says Gary.

"A game! Thank you.

Let's go play!"

Gary and Gavin play all day. They have a great time with the game.

Fun Facts

Some of the same games that you enjoy today have been around for a very long time! A game similar to checkers was being played in ancient Egypt nearly 2,600 years ago. The game of chess first appeared in India about 1,500 years ago.

You probably hope to receive gifts such as toys during holidays and for birthdays. Children in the 1800s and early 1900s usually asked for treats they could eat. Typical gifts for children in this time period included nuts, fruit, and candy. Shortly after this, teddy bears became one of the most requested gifts.

Activity

Playing a Phonics Game

If you and your friends get tired of playing checkers and board games, all you need is a pad of paper, a watch, and some pencils. Pick a phonics sound such as the sound of hard g. Next, set a time limit of five minutes. See who can come up with the longest list of words that contains that phonics sound before five minutes are up. When you are done, pick another phonics sound and start the game again!

To Learn More

Books
About the Sound of Hard G
Moncure, Jane Belk. *My "g" Sound Box®*. Mankato, MN: The Child's World, 2009.

About Games
Krensky, Stephen, and A. A. Milne. *Pooh Invents a New Game*. New York: Puffin, 2003.
Steele, Philip. *Toys and Games*. New York: Franklin Watts, 1999.
Van Allsburg, Chris. *Jumanji*. Boston: Houghton Mifflin Co., 1981.

About Gifts
Brumbeau, Jeff, and Gail De Marcken (illustrator). *Quiltmaker's Gift*. Duluth, MN: Pfeifer-Hamilton Publishers, 2000.
Kromhout, Rindert, and Annemarie van Haeringen (illustrator). *Little Donkey and the Birthday Present*. New York: NorthSouth Books, 2007.
Varley, Susan. *Badger's Parting Gifts*. New York: Lothrop, Lee & Shepard Books, 1984.

Web Sites
Visit our home page for lots of links about the Sound of Hard G:
childsworld.com/links

Note to Parents, Teachers, and Librarians: We routinely check our Web links to make sure they're safe, active sites—so encourage your readers to check them out!

Hard G
Feature Words

Proper Names

Gary

Gavin

Feature Words in Initial Position

game

gate

get

gift

give

glad

going

good

got

great

About the Authors

Joanne Meier, PhD, has worked as an elementary school teacher, university professor, and researcher. She earned her BA in early childhood education from the University of South Carolina, and her MEd and PhD in education from the University of Virginia. She currently works as a literacy consultant for schools and private organizations. Joanne lives in Virginia with her husband Eric, daughters Kella and Erin, two cats, and a gerbil.

Cecilia Minden, PhD, is the former director of the Language and Literacy Program at the Harvard Graduate School of Education. She is now a reading consultant for school and library publications. She earned her PhD in reading education from the University of Virginia. Cecilia and her husband, Dave Cupp, live outside Chapel Hill, North Carolina. They enjoy sharing their love of reading with their grandchildren, Chelsea and Qadir.

About the Illustrator

Bob Ostrom has been illustrating children's books for nearly twenty years. A graduate of the New England School of Art & Design at Suffolk University, Bob has worked for such companies as Disney, Nickelodeon, and Cartoon Network. He lives in North Carolina with his wife Melissa and three children, Will, Charlie, and Mae.